Rip van Winkle and
The Legend of Sleepy Hollow

Washington Irving

Simplified by Michael West

Illustrated by Richard Rose

Longman

| 850 word |
| vocabulary |

LONGMAN GROUP LIMITED
Longman House, Burnt Mill, Harlow,
Essex CM20 2JE, England
Associated companies throughout the world.
This edition © The estate of Michael West 1966, 1977

First published 1966
Second edition 1977
Seventh impression 1985

ISBN 0 582 53530 1

Produced by Longman Group (FE) Ltd
Printed in Hong Kong

Contents

Words outside the vocabulary for Stage 2
and are listed at the end of the book

*The children followed him whenever he walked
about the village*

Rip van Winkle

The story

This story was found among the papers of an old gentleman who lived in New York.

The Catskill mountains are about 250 kilometres north of New York.

At the foot of the Catskill mountains in the year 1765 there was a village. The people of that village were Dutch. They had come from Europe a long time ago and made their home there. Their houses were just like the houses in which they lived in Europe, and their dress was the same as the dress of the people in Holland, their home country.

Rip van Winkle

Rip van Winkle lived in one of the houses in that village. He was a very simple and kind man. He was a friend and helper to all the people in the village.

Rip's wife was very unkind to him, but he did not get angry with her. He did everything that she told him to do, but he kept away from her as much as he could. Perhaps he was so kind to others because she was so unkind to him. All the people of the village loved him, and the children were very happy with him. He played with them; he made things for them; he told them long stories. The children followed him whenever he walked about in the village.

Rip did not like work. He was not really lazy. He worked very hard at the things that he liked doing: he used to sit all day on a wet rock catching fish: he used to walk all day up hills and in the forests with his gun.

Rip and his wife

Rip worked very hard helping a friend to gather his corn, or to build a wall. He helped the women in their gardens or cleaning their houses, or carrying home things from the shop, or doing anything that their men were too lazy to do for them.

He was ready to do anyone's work, but not his own. He did not keep his own land and his garden in order. Long grass grew in his fields; his cow got into the garden and ate the plants. He did not keep his family in order. The children's clothes were old and dirty. His son, Rip, had the oldest and dirtiest clothes of them all.

But Rip was always happy. His wife talked and talked angrily at him all day; she talked about his laziness and the way he treated his family; but he did not answer, and so she went on talking—and he went outside the house.

Rip had a dog named Wolf. Rip's wife did not like Wolf: she drove him out of the house and threw things at him. Wolf did not like Mrs van Winkle.

The village inn

There was an inn in the village: it was called "King George the Third" and there was a picture of King George outside. The men of the village used to sit outside the inn, drinking and talking. There was Derick Brummel, the schoolteacher; he was very wise and used long words. There was Nicholas Vedder, the innkeeper; he sat there all day with a long pipe in his mouth. He moved along the seat to keep out of the hot sun, so you could tell the time by where he was sitting. Rip used to go and sit there to get away from his home, but his wife drove him away from there. So Rip used to take his gun and go away into the forest with his dog, Wolf.

Up the mountain side

One afternoon Rip went on and on through the forest till he came to the foot of one of the highest Catskill mountains. He went up—and up. At last he felt tired and sat down on a little grassy hill. Through an opening in the trees he could see down as far as the Hudson River. It was a beautiful sight.

The men of the village sat outside the inn

The sun was going down and the river looked like gold.

The Hudson River got its name from Captain Henry Hudson. He was an Englishman. Captain Hudson with his Dutch seamen reached the river in his ship in 1610 and wanted to stay there all the winter; but his men did not want to stay. They put him and eight other seamen in a small boat, and then sailed away, leaving the nine men there.

Rip sat down on a little grassy hill. After a time he fell asleep.

A strange-looking man

At last Rip awoke. 'Oh!' he said, 'It's late. It'll be dark before I can get back to the village, and my wife will be very angry with me. I must start to go back at once!'

He stood up. He was starting to go back when he heard a voice calling, 'Rip van Winkle! Rip van Winkle!' He looked round, but he could see only a bird flying across the mountain.

'That wasn't a real voice!' he said. 'I only thought that I heard it.' He turned to go down, but he heard the same cry again; 'Rip van Winkle! Rip van Winkle!' Wolf, his dog, was afraid: it made an angry noise and came close to Rip's side.

Rip, too, felt afraid. He looked down, and he saw a strange–looking person coming up among the rocks: Rip had never seen anyone quite like him. He was carrying some heavy thing on his back.

'Who can this person be?' Rip wondered. 'No one comes here. But perhaps it's one of the people in the village needing help.' So he went quickly down.

Between the rocks

As Rip came nearer he was very surprised at what he saw. He saw a short, square, old man with long hair and a long beard. His hair was nearly white, but his clothes were like the clothes that Dutchmen wore in the year 1600.

The old man was carrying a small barrel on his back. Rip took it and carried it for him. They climbed up a narrow place. As they went up, Rip heard a deep sound—a long, rolling sound like the sound of big guns, or like thunder. (But there was no rain, and there were no thunder clouds.)

As they went on, Rip saw two big rocks in front; the sound seemed to come from the other side of them.

'Why,' Rip wondered, 'why is he carrying that little barrel up the mountain? Why? Where is he going?' But Rip was afraid to ask. They went between the rocks and came to a small open space. It was shut in by high rocks on all sides, and trees grew down over it, hiding the sky.

The strange-looking men

There were some strange-looking people in this place. They were dressed like the old man whom Rip had met—like Dutchmen of the year 1600. Their faces were strange: one man had a very big head and very small eyes; another had a very big nose so that his face seemed to be all nose! They all had beards. There was one man who seemed to be their captain. He was fat and round. He had a fine long coat, a high hat with a feather, and his shoes were high at the back with a rose on the front.

They were playing a game of ninepins. None of them spoke, but they rolled the balls at the nine pins, and the noise of the balls made a sound like thunder among the high hills.

Rip takes a drink

As Rip and the old man came near, the men stopped playing. They stood and looked at Rip; it was such a cold dead look, with unchanging eyes, that Rip was filled with fear. The old man pointed to the barrel and showed Rip that he must give drinks to all the men. He did that. They drank; then they started to play again.

When no one was looking, Rip gave himself a drink from the barrel. It was very strong, but very good. He took another drink—and another—and

They were playing a game called ninepins

another. Yes! It was very strong! His eyes closed: he
fell into a deep sleep.

Waking up

Rip woke up. He was on the little grassy hill from
which he first saw the strange old man. It was a nice
sunny morning. The birds were flying about among
the trees.

'Oh!' thought Rip, 'Have I slept here all night?'

Then he remembered the things that happened
before he fell asleep. He remembered the old man
with his barrel, the high rocks, the little open space
where those men were playing ninepins—and the
drink. 'Oh! that drink! It was strong! What shall I
say to my wife?'

He looked round to find his gun. In place of the
good, well-oiled gun he saw a very old gun; the
metal was red as if it had been there in the rain for
years, and the wooden part was soft and full of holes.

'Those old men have done this!' he thought.
'They gave me too much to drink and then stole
my gun.'

Poor fool!

Then he looked round: 'Where's Wolf?' He called,
'Wolf! Wolf!' but Wolf did not come.

'I'll go back to that place and make those old men give me back my dog and my gun.'

He found it hard to walk: his legs were painful. At last he came to the place where he had climbed up with the old man.

It was hard work to climb up the hill because of the trees and plants through which he had to cut his way. At last he reached the two big rocks.

'We went between them,' he said. But he could not find any opening.

Rip stood there. He called again, 'Wolf! Wolf!' but there was no answer, only the cries of birds flying up above. 'Poor fool! Poor fool!' they seemed to say.

'What shall I do?' said Rip. 'It's getting late and I've had no food. I must leave Wolf and my own gun. Wolf will find food up here in the mountains.'

He took up the old gun and went back home.

Strange people

As Rip came nearer to the village he met a number of people, but he did not know any of them.

'That's strange!' he said. 'I thought that I knew everyone in the village and in the country all round it.'

Their clothes were strange—not like the dress of the people whom he knew. They looked at him. They seemed surprised and put up their hands to their faces.

'Why do they all put up their hands to their faces?' he wondered.

He put up his hand to his face, and he found that his beard was a foot long.

He came to the village. Children ran after him, shouting at him and pointing at his beard. They were strange children, strangely dressed. None of them were children whom he knew; those children were all his friends, but these children were not.

He knew all the dogs in the village—in his village. But these dogs didn't know him; they weren't friendly; they made angry noises at him and would not let him touch them.

A changed village

The village was changed. It was bigger. There were more people in it. There were many houses he had never seen before, and the old houses that he knew had gone. There were strange names over the doors, strange faces at the windows. Everything was strange.

'Isn't this my village? Isn't this the village I was born in?—the village that I left only yesterday?'

He looked up: 'There are the Catskill mountains; there's the silver Hudson River—everything just as it has always been! That drink last night has done something to my mind!'

After some time he found his way to his own
house. He went up to it very quietly because he was
afraid he would hear the angry voice of his wife.
But the windows were broken; there was no door.
There was a dog which looked like Wolf, but its
bones showed through its side; it was dirty and
unfed.

Rip called it, but it looked at him and then ran
away.

'Even my dog doesn't remember me!'

An empty house

He went into the house. His wife had always kept it
very clean, with everything in its right place. But
there was nothing there—no chairs, tables—
nothing. It was not lived in now; it had not been
lived in for a long time.

He called for his wife and children. But there was
no answer. He called again 'Wife! Wife! Answer
me.' But there was no answer. He called his son,
who was also called Rip. He called, 'Rip, my boy!
...My boy, answer me!' But there was no answer.

He went quickly away. 'I'll go to the inn. My
friends there will tell me what has happened. They
will tell me where my wife and children are, and
what has happened to my house.'

But the inn was not there! It had gone! In its

place he saw a big wooden house. It had a new name. There was a notice over the door:

THE UNION HOTEL
Jonathan Doolittle

George Washington

The great tree which grew in front of the George Inn had gone. There was a high post where it had grown, and on the post there was a flag with strange marks and lines on it. He looked for the picture of King George; but this too was changed. King George had a red coat, but the coat was now blue, and instead of a crown he had a hat. Under the picture he saw the words

GEORGE WASHINGTON

There were some people round the door of the inn, but Rip did not know any of them. And they were not like the people he used to meet at the inn. His people were quiet, slow, sleepy people; but these were making a lot of noise, talking quickly and in high voices. No! These were not like his friends.

He looked at the people. 'Where's Nicholas Vedder?' he thought. 'Where's Nicholas Vedder with his long pipe? And where's Derick Brummel, the schoolteacher, with his long words?'

There was a small man with a dried-up face and a lot of papers in his pocket. He was talking about things that Rip had never heard of—about the People's Rights, and an election—about electing a man to go to 'Congress'.

'What is "Congress"?' Rip wondered. 'Is it a thing?—or a place? And why send a man there?'

And then the little man talked about a war: 'the war of seventy-six'.

'Does he mean 1676?' Rip asked himself. 'But that was a long time back; and 1776—that is a long time in front. What war is he talking about?'

The men sitting in front of the inn looked at Rip —his long beard, his old and useless gun, his strange-looking clothes, and the women and children following him.

The little man came to him and said, 'On which side are you?'

'Side of what?' asked Rip.

'Which side do you want to win the election?'

'Election?' said Rip.

'Whom do you want to send to Congress to make laws and rule our country?'

Rip did not understand.

'Which side do you want to win the election?'

'Who is he?'

Then a rich old gentleman in fine clothes and a high hat came. He said, 'Get out of my way!' as he moved through the people.

He looked at Rip. Then he said in a deep voice: 'Why have you come to the election carrying a gun?—And who are all these people following you? Have you come to cause a fight?'

'No! No! No!' said Rip. 'I'm a poor man, a quiet man, and King George is my king. God save the King!'

'King George!' cried all the people. 'Take him away! Away! He's not an American. Who is he? Call the police!'

'Why have you come here?' said the rich old gentleman. 'Are you looking for someone? For whom?'

'I'm looking for some of my friends who come to this inn. They used to come, but I can't see any of them here.'

'Does no one here know Rip van Winkle?'

'Who are these friends of yours? What are their names?' said the rich old gentleman.

'Well—' said Rip. 'Where's Nicholas Vedder?'

'Nicholas Vedder!' said the old man. 'He died eighteen years ago.'

'Where's Brom Dutcher?'

'He went into the army at the beginning of the war, and he was killed in a battle—or lost at sea. I don't know which, but he never came back.'

'Where's Derick Brummel, the schoolteacher?'

'He went to the war, too. He did well and now he's in Congress. He's a Congressman.'

Rip did not know what to think or what to do. 'All these changes in my home and in my friends! I'm alone, alone in a strange world in which no one knows me! Does no one here know Rip van Winkle?' he cried.

'*Who am I?*'

'Oh! Rip van Winkle!' cried two or three people. 'Yes! He's there—sitting under that tree. That's Rip van Winkle.'

Rip looked. He saw someone just like himself as he was when he went up the mountain—just the same lazy young man in old and dirty clothes.

'Is that me? . . . Then who am I? I'm not myself. That's me! Someone has got into my shoes. I was myself last night, but I fell asleep on the mountain, and they have changed my gun, and everything is changed. I'm changed and I can't tell what my name is, or who I am!'

The people began to look at each other. They touched their heads: 'Is he right in his mind? Is he safe with that gun?' The rich old gentleman went away: he seemed to think that it was not safe to stay there.

Just then a pretty young woman came to take a look at this strange man with a long beard. She had a small boy in her arms; the child was afraid of the old man, and began to cry.

'Quiet, Rip!' she said. 'You little fool, the old man won't hurt you.'

The woman had called the child 'Rip'!

'I seem to remember her,' thought Rip—the old Rip. 'I remember her voice and the way she speaks. . . . What is your name?' he asked.

'Judith Gardiner.'

Rip finds a daughter

'And what was your father's name?' asked Rip.

'Ah! Poor man! His name was Rip van Winkle. But twenty years ago he went away from his home with his gun, and he has never been seen since then. His dog came home without him. No one knows if he shot himself, or was carried away by the Indians. I was only a little girl then.'

Rip wanted to ask one more question. 'Your mother? . . . Where's your mother?'

'She died a short time ago. She got very angry with a man selling things at the door, and she fell down dead.'

'Ah!' thought Rip. 'So I am safe from my wife!'

He caught his daughter in his arms. 'I'm your father!' he said. 'I was young Rip van Winkle once, but I am old Rip van Winkle now. Does no one know poor old Rip van Winkle.'

What a story!

'Does no one know Rip van Winkle?' he said again.

There was no answer. Then a very old woman came out from among them. She came close and looked into his face. 'Yes,' she said. 'That's right! He *is* Rip van Winkle. So you've come home at last. Where have you been for the past twenty years?'

Rip told his story. It did not take long to tell because all these twenty years had been to him only one night. The people looked at each other when they heard it. Some said, 'What a story! Does he think that we'll believe it?'

The rich old gentleman saw that it was safe to come back. 'No,' he said, 'we can't believe that story.'

Then they saw old Peter Vanderdonk coming along the road.

Peter Vanderdonk

Old Peter Vanderdonk came nearer.

'Let's ask him,' they said.

Peter Vanderdonk was the oldest man in the village, and he knew all the things that had happened there and all the stories that had been passed on from father to son and on and on for more years than anyone could remember.

'Yes,' he said. 'My grandfather knew all about the Catskill mountains, and he said that strange things happened there. Henry Hudson comes back to the river with his eight men every twenty years. He comes to keep watch over the great river which he was the first to find. And my father once saw them in their old Dutch clothes playing ninepins up in the mountains; and the sound of the balls was like thunder.'

Rip finds a home

The people went away. The women went to their homes and the men went on with their election. Rip's daughter took him home to live with her. She had a nice house. She had married one of those boys for whom Rip once made things.

Rip's son was very like his father—he worked hard at anything that he liked doing, but he did not like doing work on his own land.

Rip went on living as he had done in the past. Many of his friends were very old and he found friends among the younger people: they liked him very much.

'Yes,' he said. 'My grandfather knew all about the
Catskill mountains'

The end

Rip went back to his place outside the inn, and the men liked hearing his stories about the old times 'before the war'; but things which had happened after the war all seemed very strange to him, and he didn't care who ruled the country or who made laws and gave orders. The only thing he didn't like was being ruled by a wife, and now he was free of that! He could go out and come back home whenever he wanted.

He used to tell his story to every traveller who came to Mr Doolittle's inn. At first the story wasn't always quite the same, but after a time it became just the story that I have written in this book. Some always said that it wasn't true and that Rip had been out of his mind. But the old Dutch people all believed it, and, whenever they heard thunder they said, 'Ah! That's Henry Hudson and his men playing ninepins.' And there were some men whose wives were like Mrs van Winkle and they wished that they might have a drink from that barrel and wake up twenty years later.

The Legend of Sleepy Hollow

Greensburgh

The village named Greensburgh is near the Hudson
River. Two miles from the village there is a little
valley between two hills. The valley was called
Sleepy Hollow.

Sleepy Hollow was one of the quietest places in
the world. A little river runs through it with a
gentle sound which might send one to sleep.

The people of Greensburgh believed that there
was a ghost in Sleepy Hollow. It was the ghost of a
headless man riding a horse—a soldier whose head
had been shot off in a battle in Sleepy Hollow. His
body was buried just outside the church, in the
churchyard. But every night he rode out to Sleepy
Hollow along all the roads, looking for his head,
and before daylight he rode back to the church
where his body was buried.—That was the story.

Ichabod Crane

About the year 1800 a man named Ichabod Crane
had a school near Sleepy Hollow. He had long arms,
long legs and very big feet. His head was small with
very big ears and a long nose, and he looked as if he
never had enough to eat.

...he rode back to the church where his body was buried

The school stood alone at the foot of a hill covered with trees. The low sound of the children's voices could be heard, like the sound of bees, as they learned their lessons. Sometimes the voice of Ichabod Crane was heard giving orders—or there was the sound *'Smack! Smack!'* as he dealt with a lazy boy, or one who had behaved badly.

When the school closed, Ichabod often played with the larger boys. On half-days he walked home with some of the smaller boys—those who had pretty older sisters, or whose mothers were good cooks.

Ichabod's life

All the people in that place were farmers. Ichabod got very little money from the school, but he stayed at the houses of the farmers whose children came to the school. He went round them, staying a week with each, carrying everything that he owned in a red cloth. While he was staying with a farmer, he always helped on the farm. He helped to cut the corn; he took the horses to water; he drove the cows in from the field.

He also taught singing, and he was the leader of the singers in the church. The women thought that he was a very wise man. He had read a few books. He had a big book written by a man called Mather; it was about ghosts. Ichabod believed all the stories in this book. As he walked back in the evening to the farmhouse in which he was staying, every strange sound filled him with fear, and he sang the prayers that he sang in church to keep himself safe from ghosts and all such things.

Katrina

Katrina van Tassel was one of those who came to his singing lessons. She was the daughter of a rich farmer named Baltus van Tassel. She was eighteen years old and very pretty. Ichabod looked at her with loving eyes, and he looked at her father's big house, his rich fields, his fine animals, and the food in his kitchen.

'How can I win Katrina to be my wife?' That was what he thought as he looked at her—and the house and the farm. 'Ah! How?' Ichabod was not the only man, and Katrina liked to play with the men; sometimes she was nice to one man and he thought he might be winning—and then she seemed to like another.

Among the men there was one named Brom. Brom was very big and strong. He was a very good rider and knew a great deal about horses. Everyone liked him. If there was any fight, or anything that would make him laugh, he was always there. He had three or four close friends; he was their leader.

Brom also wanted to win Katrina. His horse was

often seen outside Van Tassel's house on a Sunday evening.

Brom

As singing teacher, Ichabod could go to the farm as often as he liked. He sat with Katrina under the big tree at the river side, or walked with her in the moonlight. He seemed to be winning, and Brom's horse was not seen outside the house on Sundays.

Brom would have liked to fight Ichabod for the lady, as men did long ago and in the story books; but Ichabod was a quiet man, and was careful not to quarrel with Brom or let him have any reason for fighting him. Brom tried to make Ichabod angry by going into the school at night and throwing the chairs and tables and everything about. He taught his dog to make strange noises and said to Katrina, 'My dog can sing better than Ichabod.' But it was no use! Ichabod would not fight. Brom said, 'I must think of some other way.'

Gunpowder

One day a servant came to the school to ask Ichabod to come to a meal at Van Tassel's house that evening.

Ichabod finished the school work very quickly and sent the boys away. He was staying at Hans van

Ripper's farm. He went back to the farm, put on his best clothes and said to Van Ripper, 'May I use your horse?'

Van Ripper was a great horseman, and loved riding as fast as he could across the country. Many years ago a horse named Gunpowder was his best horse; but Gunpowder was now very old and only did work on the farm. He had only one eye but in that one eye you could sometimes see the fire which had made him Van Ripper's best-loved horse long ago.

Van Ripper said, 'Oh yes: you may ride Gunpowder. Gunpowder was a very good horse once, very fast, and rather dangerous, but he's very quiet now.'

At Van Tassel's house

So Ichabod rode on Gunpowder, and in the evening reached Van Tassel's house. All the farmers of the country were there, with their wives and sons and daughters. Brom was there too. He had come on his best horse—a dangerous animal which only Brom could ride.

They all sat down to a big meal. The table was covered with food. Ichabod looked at all this fine food. As he ate and drank more and more he thought, 'Ha! One day all this will be mine and I'll laugh at Van Ripper with his little farm and his old broken-down horse, and I won't ask the poor schoolteacher to come and have a meal among my grand friends.'

After that they went into the big hall and danced. Ichabod thought that he was a very good dancer. He danced with Katrina and gave her loving looks as he did so. Brom sat angrily alone near the door: he couldn't dance.

Ghost stories

When the dance ended, Ichabod went and sat with Van Tassel and some of the older people outside. They were telling stories about old times—and about ghosts. One man told a story about the ghost of a woman dressed in white which was seen near the big tree in Sleepy Hollow. She had killed herself near that tree. There was a story of Captain André who was shot at the crossing over the river not far from the tree. But the best stories were about the Headless Horseman.

Several people said that they had heard him. Some said that he put his horse in the churchyard every night. A man called Brower said that once he met the horseman on his way back from Sleepy Hollow; the horseman made him get up behind him on his horse and rode over hill and valley until he came to the bridge, and there he threw Brower into the water. That was the story.

He danced with Katrina

Brom laughed. He said, 'I can tell a better story. One night I was coming back near Sleepy Hollow and the Horseman came up behind me. I said, "Come! Let's see which horse can go faster, yours or mine." I should have won because my horse was much faster; but, just as we came to the bridge near the church, there was a noise like thunder—and he had gone! I couldn't see him any more.'

The white thing

Ichabod heard these stories, and he himself told other stories from Mather's book.

The farmers and their wives and daughters began to go away; but Ichabod stayed so as to talk to Katrina. He thought, 'This is the time to ask her to marry me. Now I shall win her!'

I don't know what happened at that meeting between Ichabod and Katrina; but Ichabod came away looking very sad. He got on to his horse and started to ride home—to Van Ripper's farm; and, as he rode, he thought about all the ghost stories that he had been hearing and telling.

The night became darker and darker. He was now near Sleepy Hollow. There was a big tree there. He thought that he saw something—some white thing!—in it. He heard a strange deep sound: was it made by the wind, or was it the voice of a ghost? Was that white thing only a dead part of the tree? He rode quickly on.

32

At the river

Ichabod rode on and came to the crossing over the river. Here he had to ride Gunpowder through the water.

On the other side of the river there were some big trees which made a dark shadow over the water. Captain André was shot just here. This was the place where his ghost was seen. No one liked to come here after dark.

Ichabod was afraid. He hit his horse so as to make it go across quickly, but it turned away to the side. He hit it again but it went to the other side. Ichabod was angry; he hit the horse again and again; it moved on; then it stopped so that Ichabod nearly went over its head.

Then Ichabod heard a sound and in the dark shadow of the trees on the other side he saw something big. It stood high up above him. It did not move. It seemed to be waiting—waiting to jump out on him!

The Thing

What should Ichabod do? It was too late to turn back; and, if he did turn back, that Thing would follow him, and come faster than he could ride.

'Who are you?' he said.

There was no answer.

Ichabod nearly went over its head

'What are you?'

Still no answer.

He shut his eyes and sang a prayer.

The Thing moved: it jumped out into the road. Ichabod opened his eyes. The night was very dark but he could just see a Thing which looked like a horseman on a big black horse.

Ichabod rode on—keeping to one side of the road, the side on which Gunpowder's one good eye was: so Gunpowder could not see the Horseman. Ichabod thought of Brom's story about the Headless Horseman, how Brom rode fast and left the Horseman behind. He made Gunpowder go faster; but the Horseman came on faster and stayed at his side. He stopped: the Horseman stopped. He went on again; the Horseman came on.

He tried to sing, but no voice came from his dry mouth.

The Headless Horseman

Then Ichabod came to some rising ground and he saw the Horseman against the sky. He was headless; he was carrying his head in front of him on the saddle. Ichabod hit Gunpowder again—and again —and again. Gunpowder jumped and went on faster. The life and fire which it had known long ago came back. Faster! Faster!

The road to Van Ripper's farm went to one side;

but Gunpowder went down the road to the other side—the road which led downhill to the bridge where the Headless Horseman threw Brower into the water, and then on to the church, where the Headless Horseman was buried.

Ichabod loses his saddle

Ichabod and Gunpowder went down the hill; the Horseman was behind. Ichabod thought, 'Perhaps I have left the Horseman behind and have got away safely—as Brom did.' But, just as Ichabod was half-way down the hill, something broke and the saddle turned round under Ichabod. Ichabod put his arms round the horse's head; the saddle fell to the ground and he heard the other horse go over it. 'Oh!' he thought, 'that was Van Ripper's best saddle! He will be so angry.'

Ichabod stayed on Gunpowder's back. The bridge was now quite near. He could see the white walls of the church through the trees. Brom had said that the Horseman left him here: Brom said 'Then there was a sound like thunder—and he had gone. I couldn't see him any more.' That was what Brom said. 'Perhaps,' thought Ichabod, 'that will happen here, at the bridge, and I shall be saved! If I can reach the bridge I'll be safe.'

The Horseman's head

Ichabod heard the Horseman close behind him. He reached the bridge; he was on the bridge; he reached the other side. Then he looked back to see if the Horseman was still there. He was still there! He was standing up across his saddle and he had some big thing in his hands. He was throwing it! He threw his head at Ichabod. It hit Ichabod and he fell to the ground, and Gunpowder went on, leaving him there.

On the next morning Gunpowder was found, without his saddle, at Van Ripper's farm. The boys waited for Ichabod at the school. He did not come. They waited all the morning; no Ichabod!

School time ended and Ichabod did not come back to Van Ripper's house.

The pumpkin

'Where is Ichabod?' said Van Ripper. 'And where's my saddle?'

He set out with all his men to find them. They followed the marks on the ground. In the road to the church they found the saddle, dirty and broken.

They came to the bridge, and the stream. On the other side of the bridge they found Ichabod's hat and close to it a broken pumpkin.

But they did not find a body.

*...they found Ichabod's hat and close to it
a broken pumpkin*

Next Sunday all the people came to the place: they said, 'He has been carried off by the Headless Horseman.'

Brom laughs

Some years later an old farmer came back from New York. He said, 'I saw Ichabod Crane. He went away because Katrina would not marry him, and because he was afraid of Van Ripper's anger about his saddle, and because of the Headless Horseman.'

'What happened to him after he left here?' asked Katrina—now married to Brom.

'He started a school. He learned law and was elected to Congress. He became a Congressman....'

'Why was a pumpkin found there?' asked Katrina. 'How did that get there?'

Brom laughed.

Questions

Rip van Winkle
The story
1 Where are the Catskill mountains?
2 What part of Europe did the people come from?

Rip van Winkle
1 Was Rip van Winkle a kind, or unkind man?
2 What did Rip take with him in the forest?

Rip and his wife
1 What work didn't Rip do?
2 What was the name of Rip's dog?

The village inn
1 What was the name of the inn?
2 Who drove Rip away from the inn?

Up the mountain side
1 What could Rip see through an opening in the trees?
2 In what year did Captain Hudson reach the river?
3 How many men were left with Captain Hudson?

A strange-looking man
1 What did Rip hear?
2 What did Wolf do?

Between the rocks
1 What colour was the man's hair?
2 The sound was like——. Like what?

The strange-looking men
1 How were the men dressed? Like...
2 What game were they playing?

Rip takes a drink
1 What did Rip do when no one was looking?
2 What did Rip do after that?

40

Waking up
1 Where was Rip when he awoke?
2 What time was it?
3 What did Rip see in place of his gun?

Poor fool!
1 What did Rip call?
2 What made it hard to climb up the hill?
3 Why didn't Rip go between the rocks?

Strange people
1 What did the people do when they looked at Rip?
2 What did the dogs do?

A changed village
1 Why did Rip go to his house quietly?
2 What did the dog do?

An empty house
1 What was the name of Rip's son?
2 What was the new name of the inn?

George Washington
1 What was in the place of the great tree?
2 Whose picture was in the place of King George?

An election
1 What was the small man talking about?
2 What war did the little man talk about?

'Who is he?'
1 What did the rich old gentleman ask Rip?
2 What words made the people angry?

'Does no one here know Rip van Winkle?'
1 When did Nicholas Vedder die?
2 When did Brom Dutcher go away?
3 What is Derick Brummel now?

'Who am I?'
1 Where was the young Rip?
2 What was the name of the small boy?
3 What was the name of the woman?

Rip finds a daughter
1 Who was the woman's father?
2 With whom did Rip's wife get angry?
3 What happened to her then?

'What a story!'
1 Who said, 'Yes, that's right, he *is* Rip van Winkle!'?
2 What did she ask him? —— 'Where———?'

Peter Vanderdonk
1 Who told Peter about the Catskill mountains?
2 When does Henry Hudson come back?
3 Who once saw Henry Hudson and his men?

Rip finds a home
1 With whom did Rip live?
2 Where did Rip find friends?

The end
1 Who believed Rip's story?
2 What did the people say when they heard thunder?

The Legend of Sleepy Hollow
Greensburgh
1 What river was the village near?
2 Where was the Headless Horseman buried?
3 Why did the Horseman ride out along the roads? —— He was looking for...

Ichabod Crane
1 What was the school teacher's name?
2 What sounds came from the school?

42

Ichabod's life
1 How long did Ichabod stay with each farmer?
2 What did Ichabod also teach?
3 What was Ichabod's big book about?

Katrina
1 How old was Katrina?
2 What was her father?
3 What was the name of the other man who wanted to marry Katrina?

Brom
1 What would Brom like to do?
2 What did Brom do in the school?

Gunpowder
1 What did the servant ask Ichabod to do?
2 At whose farm was Ichabod staying?
3 What was the name of Van Ripper's old horse?

At Van Tassel's house
1 Who ate and drank more and more?
2 What did they do after they had eaten?

Ghost stories
1 Where was the Woman in White seen? —— Near...
2 Where was Captain André shot?
3 What did the Horseman do to Brower?

The white thing
1 Why did Ichabod stay? —— So as to...
2 Where did he think that he heard and saw a ghost?

At the river
1 What did the horse do when Ichabod hit it?
2 What did Ichabod see in the shadow?

The Thing
1 What did the Thing look like?
2 What did Ichabod try to do, but could not?

The Headless Horseman
1 Where did the Horseman carry his head?
2 Where was Brower thrown into the water?

Ichabod loses his saddle
1 What fell to the ground?
2 Who will be angry about the saddle?

The Horseman's head
1 What did the Horseman have in his hands?
2 What did the Horseman do with this thing?

The pumpkin
1 What did they find close to Ichabod's hat?
2 What did they not find?

Brom laughs
1 Whom did Katrina marry?
2 Why did Ichabod go away? (Three reasons.)
3 What did Ichabod become?

List of extra words

barrel *a round wooden case to hold drink*
bury, buried *put (a dead person's body) into the ground*
churchyard *the ground round a church*
elect *choose a person (at an election) to speak for you in the House that makes laws*
ghost *a dead person seen by living people*
inn *a house where they sell drink and food, and where travellers can sleep*

legend *a story about the past that has been told to one after another through the years*
pumpkin *a large round yellow fruit that grows on the ground*
saddle *a place for a rider on a horse's back*
strange *unlike the things or people that you see every day*
thunder *the sound of electricity in the sky*
valley *low ground between two hills*

The people and places in the stories

The symbols shown are those of the *Dictionary of Contemporary English* (Longman)

BALTUS VAN TASSEL	/ˈbæltəs væn ˈtæsl/
BROM	/brɒm/
BROM DUTCHER	/ˈbrɒm ˈdʌtʃəʳ/
BROWER	/ˈbrəʊəʳ/
CAPTAIN ANDRÉ	/ˈkæptən ˈɒndreɪ/
CATSKILL	/ˈkætskɪl/
DERICK BRUMMEL	/ˈderɪk ˈbrʌml/
GEORGE THE THIRD	/ˈdʒɔːdʒ ðə ˈθɜːd/
GEORGE WASHINGTON	/ˈdʒɔːdʒ ˈwɒʃɪŋtn/
GREENSBURGH	/ˈgriːnzbərə/
GUNPOWDER	/ˈgʌnpaʊdəʳ/
HANS VAN RIPPER	/ˈhæns væn ˈrɪpəʳ/
ICHABOD CRANE	/ˈɪkəbɒd ˈkreɪn/
JONATHAN DOOLITTLE	/ˈdʒɒnəθn ˈduːlɪtl/
JUDITH GARDINER	/ˈdʒuːdɪθ ˈgɑːdnəʳ/
KATRINA	/kæˈtriːnə/
MATHER	/ˈmeɪðəʳ/
NICHOLAS VEDDER	/ˈnɪkələs ˈvedəʳ/
PETER VANDERDONK	/ˈpiːtə ˈvændədʊŋk/
RIP VAN WINKLE	/ˈrɪp væn ˈwɪŋkl/
SLEEPY HOLLOW	/ˈsliːpɪ ˈhɒləʊ/